Put Beginning Readers on the Right Track with
ALL ABOARD READING™

The All Aboard Reading series is especially for beginning readers. Written by noted authors and illustrated in full color, these are books that children really and truly *want* to read—books to excite their imagination, tickle their funny bone, expand their interests, and support their feelings. With five different reading levels, All Aboard Reading lets you choose which books are most appropriate for your children and their growing abilities.

Picture Readers
Picture Readers have super-simple texts, with many nouns appearing as rebus pictures. At the end of each book are 24 flash cards—on one side is the rebus picture; on the other side is the written-out word.

First Friends
First Friends, First Readers have a super-simple text starring lovable recurring characters. Each book features two easy stories that will hold the attention of even the youngest reader while promoting an early sense of accomplishment.

Level 1
Level 1 books have very few lines per page, very large type, easy words, lots of repetition, and pictures with visual "cues" to help children figure out the words on the page.

Level 2
Level 2 books are printed in slightly smaller type than Level 1 books. The stories are more complex, but there is still lots of repetition in the text, and many pictures. The sentences are quite simple and are broken up into short lines to make reading easier.

Level 3
Level 3 books have considerably longer texts, harder words, and more complicated sentences.

All Aboard for happy reading!

For Mary and her very good cat, Fiona—C.M.

For Eloise and Charlotte Lindblom—T.K.

Library of Congress Cataloging-in-Publication Data is available.

ISBN 0-448-42665-X (GB)   A   B   C   D   E   F   G   H   I   J

ISBN 0-448-42622-6 (pbk.)   A   B   C   D   E   F   G   H   I   J

ALL
ABOARD
READING™

Level 1

That Bad, Bad Cat!

By Claire Masurel
Illustrated by True Kelley

Grosset & Dunlap • New York

Once there was a cat.

The cat scratched the table.

The cat scratched the chair.

"Bad, bad cat!"
his family said.

He tore up the pillows.

He tore up the bed.

"Bad, bad cat!"
his family said.

He ate the plants.

He pulled up the flowers.

"Bad, bad cat!"
his family said.

He spilled milk.

He stole food.

"Bad, bad cat!"
his family said.

One day, the cat ran outside.

"Do not go far!"

his family said.

But he did.

He was not back for lunch.
"That bad, bad cat,"
his family said.

He was not back for dinner.
Now his family began to worry.
"Kitty! Darling! Sweetie! Honey!"
they called.
"Please come back!"

They looked all over for him.

They asked everybody,
"Have you seen our cat?"

Without him,
the house was not the same.

"I miss him."

"I miss him."

"We miss him."

Every day they left treats.

And they left a window open,

just in case.

And he did come back!

They hugged him.

They kissed him.

"You are a good, good cat.

Don't ever run away again!"

He loved them,

no matter what they said.

And they loved him . . .

no matter what he did—

that good, bad cat!